CIRCUS!

Written and illustrated by
Mattie Lou O'Kelley

For Lillie and Johnnie

The Atlantic Monthly Press
Boston   New York

It was pitch-black when Mama clapped us awake. Circus day! "Hurry up, sleepyheads. Time to feed the chickens and water the mules."

Johnnie pulled the covers over his head. "What are the others doing?"

"They've been up for hours, putting up peppers and strings of leather britches to dry on the kitchen wall," Mama said.

In the kitchen Papa gave Johnnie the chicken feed
and me the lantern. Oh, was it dark outside!

Buck and Scott went with us. They weren't worth a hoot. They never barked once. I never saw so many boogers in my life. Johnnie whispered, "Let's run. Something's looking at me."

I said, "Me, too," and we shot back into the house.

We hardly got a bite of breakfast before it was time to go to school. Mama said, "Hurry home at noon and don't lose the money for the spices." On our way out we peeked in the big-girls' room: primping up!

I could hardly wait till noon. Finally I held up both hands. "Mama said to let us come home now to see the circus." It sounded bigger to use Mama's say-so.

Outside I was waving Mama's money around, feeling like a big ike, when Sandy and Jaybird whipped it out of my hands. I screamed, "Teacher, teacher," but all the kids just shot off yelling "tattle-tale." I knew what I'd get when I got home.

Johnnie and I got whipped, all right. Mama even
made us whip each other. We'd never fed the chickens or watered the mules like we were told and we'd
lost the spice money, too. What hurt most was the big
ones laughing at us — but Mama said we could still
go to the circus!

At last off we went! Buck and Scott led the way. Mama worried that she shouldn't have left the feather beds out to air. Papa said she was fiddling with the elements, for he was sure it would come up a cloud.

Papa was right.
We just made it to the
bridge when there was
the cloud, popping and
lightening to beat the
band. Papa reined in.
"We'll have to turn
back! The Pittman Bot-
toms will be flooded."
Johnnie and I were
scared cold. "But the
circus only comes once
a year," we begged.

The cloud passed over while we waited in the
bridge. The sun even came out, but when we got
down the hill, there it was — water roaring over the
road in the Pittman Bottoms. Papa took one look at
our faces. "We'll see if the horses can make it."

"We want to wade," Johnnie and I shouted.

We made it across and down the road, past Aunt
Mary's. She was out picking cotton. She never even
stopped, just hollered, "What in the name of com-
mon sense are you folks doing traipsing around with
cotton to pick?" Johnnie and I giggled like our giz-
zards were tickled. Didn't she know the circus was
coming?

Papa took us the shortcut through the graveyard. Johnnie and I kept quiet. We didn't want to see any more ghosts. All of a sudden Johnnie pointed. "There's the train coming, Papa. Let's race the train!"

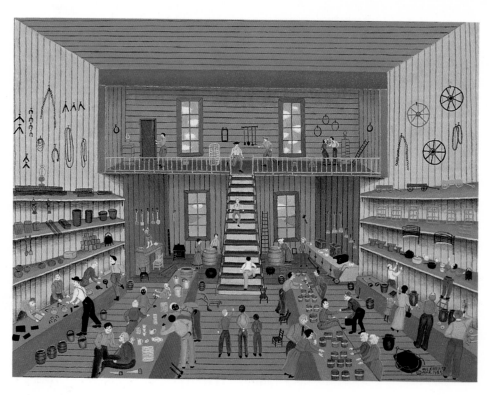

The train was already at the station when we got to town. Mama wanted to stop at the dry-goods store while Papa was in the hardware store getting plow points and mule shoes and, Mama said, "no telling what else."

"I want to get to the circus," Johnnie said real loud.

Finally we were on our way again, headed to Cousin Emmaline's for the picnic and to watch the circus parade.

We'd no sooner pulled into the yard than Cousin John let out a whoop. "Parade, parade! The circus parade is coming!"

We followed the parade right up to the circus grounds. Oh, the merry-go-round! Bells were tinkling, the horses going up and down. "Papa, Papa, can we ride? Can we ride?" I picked a white horse. We rode until our heads were spinning.

What should we do next? Papa wanted to see the elephants. He said he could use one on the farm. Willie, Tom, and Ben ran to see the snakes while Lillie, Ruth, and Gert went to have their fortunes told. Johnnie and I spent our ten cents trying to win a doll.

It was time for the show to start. Mama said real
proud, "Stand back now and let your papa do this."
Papa said, "I'll get the tickets. You young'uns get
in there fast as you can and grab a front seat."

Inside, everything was going on at once. Tumbling, music, a giant croc, and dogs running through hoops of fire. Thank goodness Buck and Scott stayed right by us! I waved my hand to make sure the popcorn man and balloon man saw us.

Johnnie hollered, "Look at the tall men! Where are they born, on the moon?"

Mama said, "Shu-sh! That's just people like us standing on Tommy Walkers."

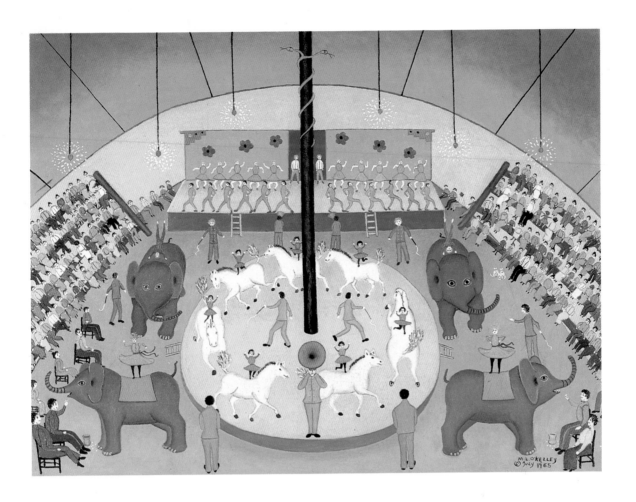

Then the elephants paraded out, followed by girls
on white horses. They didn't look any older than me!
Before we knew it, a man with a big horn announced
the show was ending. I couldn't believe it.

Happy as june bugs, we set out for home, Buck and Scott still running ahead. Lucky for us they didn't see the possum hunt and raise a ruckus.

Papa said, "Now you've seen the circus. What did you think?" Gert said she liked the outfits the dancing girls wore. Tom and Ben liked the lions.

"Did you see the snakes and monkeys on the pole?" shouted Johnnie.

"I wish I had a white pony of my own," I said.

By the time we got
home, Johnnie and I
were so sleepy that Papa
said he'd do our chores,
just this once; after all,
the circus doesn't come
to town every day.

Illustrations as they appear in the book

TEXT AND ILLUSTRATIONS COPYRIGHT © 1986 BY MATTIE LOU O'KELLEY

FIRST EDITION

LIBRARY OF CONGRESS CATALOG CARD NO. 86-3404

DNP

Published simultaneously in Canada

PRINTED IN JAPAN